WHODUNITS?™

The Case of the Vanishing House

Written by Jack Long

Illustrated by Leonard Shortall

Modern Publishing
A Division of Unisystems, Inc.
New York, New York 10022

TO AMANDA AND
STEPHEN - SHORTALL
L.S.

TO MY GRANDCHILD
NICHOLAS
C.D.L.

TO NINA AND JACK
RIESMAN
J.L.

Published by Modern Publishing,
a division of Unisystems, Inc.

Copyright © 1989 by Carlo DeLucia

TM—WHODUNITS? Mystery Storybooks is a trademark of Modern
Publishing, a division of Unisystems, Inc.

®—Honey Bear Books is a trademark of Honey Bear
Productions, Inc., and is registered in the U.S. Patent and
Trademark Office.

Printed in Belgium

TABLE OF CONTENTS

Chapter One
Nibble by Nibble

"Is this the Betty Beaver Detective Agency?"

Betty Beaver looked up from her desk and nodded.

In the doorway stood a small mouse. "My name is Elmer and I desperately need your help!"

"Whatever is the trouble?" asked Betty's assistant, Perry Possum.

Elmer Mouse looked as if he might cry. "My new house is beginning to disappear, nibble by nibble, bite by bite!"

"This I must see!" said Betty.
"I'll lead the way," said Elmer.

Perry Possum agreed to stay to look after
the agency, while Betty followed Elmer deep
into Good Forest.

"Here we are," Elmer said, as they came upon a very pretty house.

"Why, it's a gingerbread house!" Betty exclaimed.

"Yes," said Mrs. Elmer Mouse, coming out
of the front door. "Our friend, Bart Bear, the
baker, made it for us."

"It took a lot of work to move all of our things from our old house here, but our cousins helped," Elmer added. Betty Beaver looked on.

"We've already sold our old home to the Ferret family," said Mrs. Mouse. "If we don't stop the nibbler, we'll have no place to live!" She began to cry.

"There, there," said Betty, patting Mrs.
Mouse's shoulder. "Don't worry. We'll nab the
nibbler."
"How?" asked Elmer.
"I have a plan," Betty said.

"I'll need extra help to set my plan in motion," said Betty.

"We'll call our cousins," Elmer said.

The cousins arrived promptly—all four of
them.
    "I'm Edith."
    "I'm Edna."
    "I'm Edward."
    "I'm Eugene."

Chapter Two
Not a Squeak!

Soon Mrs. Mouse called them to the table.
"Apples, cheese, and chocolate chip
cookies!" the four cousins exclaimed. "Our
favorites!"

While they ate, Betty Beaver said, "Here's my plan to catch the nibbler."

"Whoever is nibbling should be back tonight," Betty told them. "You cousins hide in the bushes around the house."

"Whoever sees the nibbler will squeak a warning squeak. The rest of us will come running."

23

As the sun began to set, Edward, Eugene,
Edna and Edith hid in the bushes.

It grew dark.

Mrs. Mouse pulled down the shades and locked the doors for the night. Then she sat down to wait with Betty and Elmer.

"Didn't I hear a nibble?" Elmer asked.

"Didn't I hear a gnawing sound?" Mrs. Mouse whispered.

26

They listened for a warning squeak from
the four cousins.
Not a single squeak!

At daylight, Betty, and Mr. and Mrs. Mouse
went outside.

The four cousins were sound asleep.

Parts of the front porch were nibbled
away.

"Look at the steps!" cried Elmer. "They're eaten too, and there's a bite-sized hole in the side of the house!"

"Some *thing* is eating our house!" cried Mrs. Mouse.

"May I use your telephone?" asked Betty
Beaver.
   She called Perry Possum.

"This is a bigger mystery than I thought," she told him. "Can you come over and help me?"

Perry Possum soon arrived. Betty showed him every gnaw and nibble.

"There's more than one *thing* gnawing and nibbling," Perry said. "Several *things* are eating this house."

Perry looked at the nibbled roof shingles.
"Some *thing* is tall," he said.

He looked at the nibbles at the bottom
of the porch steps. "And some *thing* is small."

"And some *thing* gnaws," remarked Eugene and Edith.

"And some *thing* nibbles," Edna and Edward added.

"And some *thing* pecks," said Betty.

"House eaters are all around us!" cried
Mrs. Mouse.

"We must catch them," said Betty.
She looked at a tree close to the gingerbread house.

Chapter Three
Perry's Look-Out

"Perry," she said. "You can be our look-out
tonight. Climb up to the top of the tree and hide
in the branches."

For practice, Perry climbed the tree and
perched on the top branch.
"Can you see me?" he yelled.

"No," everyone shouted.

"Tonight," Betty said, "we'll catch the house eaters."

Mr. and Mrs. Mouse, the four cousins, Betty Beaver and Perry Possum had dinner. Perry helped Mrs. Mouse with the dishes, while Betty and Elmer pulled down the window shades and checked the doors.

At twilight, Perry climbed to the topmost branch of the nearby tree.

Chapter Four
They're Here!

Twilight changed to nighttime. At the top of the tree, Perry watched and listened.

Inside the house, Betty and the Mouses waited.

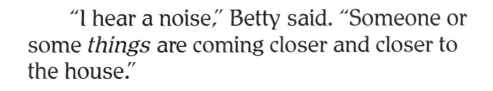

"I hear a noise," Betty said. "Someone or some *things* are coming closer and closer to the house."

"They're here!" Perry shouted.

Everyone rushed outside.

Susie and Sylvie Squirrel
nibbled on the porch.

Davy Deer chewed a shingle.

Sammy Skunk gnawed the steps.

Oliver Owl pecked at the chimney.

"Stop where you are in the name of the law!" Perry cried.

The animals swung around.

"Why are you eating the Mouses' house?" demanded Betty.

52

"The Mouses' house!" cried the animals.
"You mean someone *lives* here?"

"Of course," said Elmer. *We* do!"

"We didn't know," said Sammy. "We never
saw anyone around. We thought nobody knew
about the house but us. We work the night shift
over at the Tree Swing Factory. We get a snack
break at midnight."

"And the house tastes so good, we've been eating here every night!" said Sylvie.

Everyone stared at the nibblers in
surprise.
    Then, Elmer began to giggle, then chuckle,
then he let out a great big laugh.

Pretty soon, everyone joined in.
"Well," said Mrs. Mouse, "I'd better start
baking gingerbread to repair the holes."
"We'll help you!" said Eugene, Edith,
Edward and Edna.

The nibblers said they would make the
Mouses an extra-special tree swing to make up
for eating their house.

60

A tired Betty and Perry headed home.
"Another case solved," Perry sighed happily.
"Yes," said Betty. "And the Mouses can finally enjoy their home, *sweet*, home."